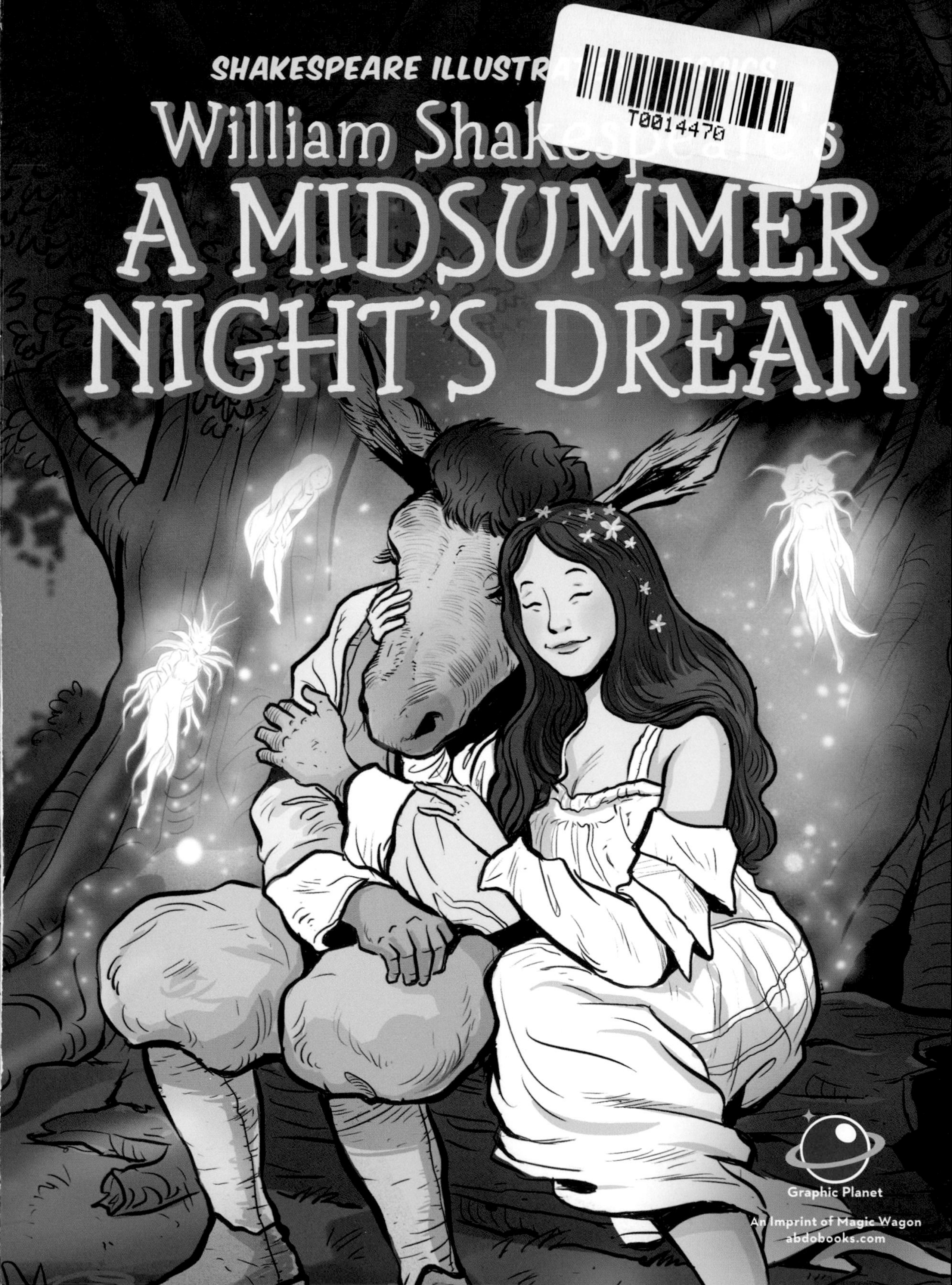

SHAKESPEARE ILLUSTRAT

# William Shakespeare's A MIDSUMMER NIGHT'S DREAM



Graphic Planet

An Imprint of Magic Wagon
abdobooks.com

abdobooks.com

Published by Magic Wagon, a division of ABDO, PO Box 398166, Minneapolis, Minnesota 55439. 

Printed in the United States of America, North Mankato, Minnesota.
052022
092022

Adapted by Daniel Conner
Cover art by Dave Shephard
Interior art by Rod Espinosa
Edited by Tamara L. Britton
Interior layout and design by Candice Keimig and Colleen McLaren

**Library of Congress Control Number: 2021952002**

**Publisher's Cataloging-in-Publication Data**

Names: Shakespeare, William; Conner, Daniel, authors. | Espinosa, Rod, illustrator.
Title: William Shakespeare's A midsummer night's dream / by William Shakespeare, Adapted by Daniel Conner; illustrated by Rod Espinosa.
Description: Minneapolis, Minnesota: Magic Wagon, 2023. | Series: Shakespeare illustrated classics
Summary: Hilarious mix-ups and mishaps befall Athens and its people when suddenly everyone is in love with the wrong person, and Fairy King Oberon does his best to untangle the mess.
Identifiers: ISBN 9781098233303 (lib. bdg.) | ISBN 9781644948446 (pbk.) | ISBN 9781098234140 (ebook) | ISBN 9781098234560 (Read-to-Me ebook)
Subjects: LCSH: Midsummer night's dream (Shakespeare, William)--Juvenile fiction. | Hippolyta (Greek mythological character)--Juvenile fiction. | Theseus, King of Athens--Juvenile fiction. | Courtship--Juvenile fiction. | Fairy plays--Juvenile fiction. | Literature--Juvenile fiction.
Classification: DDC 741.5--dc23

# Table of Contents

# Cast of Characters

**PUCK**
Oberon's jester

**THESEUS**
Duke of Athens

**HIPPOLYTA**
Queen of the Amazons

**EGEUS**
Hermia's father

**HERMIA**
Daughter of Egeus

**DEMETRIUS**
Young man of Athens

**LYSANDER**
Young man of Athens

**HELENA**
Hermia's best friend

**KING OBERON**
King of the fairies

**QUEEN TITANIA**
Queen of the fairies

**COBWEB AND PEASEBLOSSOM**
Titania's attendants

**MOTH AND MUSTARDSEED**
Titania's attendants

**PETER QUINCE**
Actor

**ROBIN STARVELING AND NICK BOTTOM**
Actors

**FRANCIS FLUTE AND SNUG**
Actors

**TOM SNOUT**
Actor

# Synopsis

Duke Theseus of Athens is preparing to marry Hippolyta, the queen of the Amazons. Egeus, an Athenian nobleman, brings his daughter Hermia, Demetrius, and Lysander to see Theseus. Egeus wants Hermia to marry Demetrius, who loves her. But she refuses because she loves Lysander. Egeus wants Hermia punished for disobeying his will. Theseus gives Hermia until his wedding day to decide what to do. Refusing her father's wishes could result in her death.

Hermia and Lysander leave Athens and travel to Lysander's aunt's house where they plan to marry. They shared their plan with Hermia's friend Helena. Demetrius had been engaged to Helena, but had left her for Hermia. Helena tells Demetrius Hermia's plan, hoping to regain his love. But Demetrius takes off through a forest after the two, and Helena follows him.

Fairy king Oberon and Titania his queen are in the forest. Titania has just returned from India to bless Theseus and Hippolyta's wedding. She brought an Indian prince with her. Oberon wants to make the boy a knight. Titania refuses, and Oberon plans revenge. He sends Puck to get a magical flower. When juice from the flower is spread on a sleeping person's eyes, he or she will fall in love with the first thing he or she sees upon awakening.

Oberon wants the flower's juice spread on Titania's eyes. Since Demetrius has been cruel to Helena, Oberon tells Puck to spread the liquid on his eyes too. Puck accidentally puts the juice on Lysander. Lysander awakens, sees Helena, and falls in love with her. In trying to correct his mistake, Puck causes both Demetrius and Lysander to love Helena. Hermia is jealous and challenges Helena to a fight. Demetrius and Lysander are about to fight too, but Puck lures them away and they become lost.

When Titania awakes, the first person she sees is Bottom, one of a group of Athenian actors rehearsing a play in the forest. Puck has changed Bottom's head into that of a donkey, but Titania dotes on him. Puck spies the sleeping Lysander and spreads the flower's juice on his eyes. Lysander awakens to see Hermia. Theseus and Hippolyta find everyone in the forest, and they all return to Athens. The wedding becomes a group event at which three couples marry. The Athenian actors perform their play, and later when everyone is asleep, the fairies bless the sleeping couples.

In Athens, Greece, at the palace of Duke Theseus...
FAIR HIPPOLYTA, OUR NUPTIAL HOUR DRAWS ON APACE. FOUR HAPPY DAYS BRING IN ANOTHER MOON. BUT O, METHINKS HOW SLOW THIS OLD MOON WANES!
FOUR DAYS WILL QUICKLY STEEP THEMSELVES IN NIGHT, FOUR NIGHTS WILL QUICKLY DREAM AWAY THE TIME.
HIPPOLYTA, I WOOED THEE WITH MY SWORD. BUT I WILL WED THEE IN ANOTHER KEY, WITH POMP, WITH TRIUMPH, AND WITH REVELING.

HAPPY BE THESEUS, OUR RENOWNED DUKE!
THANKS, GOOD EGEUS. WHAT'S THE NEWS WITH THEE?
FULL OF VEXATION COME I, WITH COMPLAINT...
...AGAINST MY CHILD, MY DAUGHTER HERMIA.
STAND FORTH, DEMETRIUS. MY NOBLE LORD, THIS MAN HATH MY CONSENT TO MARRY HER.
STAND FORTH, LYSANDER. AND MY GRACIOUS DUKE, THIS HATH BEWITCHED THE BOSOM OF MY CHILD.
SHE WILL NOT HERE BEFORE YOUR GRACE CONSENT TO MARRY WITH DEMETRIUS. AS SHE IS MINE, I MAY DISPOSE OF HER WHICH SHALL BE EITHER TO THIS GENTLEMAN OR TO HER DEATH.

WHAT SAY YOU, HERMIA? DEMETRIUS IS A WORTHY GENTLEMAN.
SO IS LYSANDER!
BY THE NEXT NEW MOON EITHER PREPARE TO WED DEMETRIUS...
... OR ELSE TO DIE FOR DISOBEDIENCE TO YOUR FATHER'S WILL!

HOW NOW, MY LOVE? THE COURSE OF TRUE LOVE NEVER DID RUN SMOOTH!

IF THEN TRUE LOVERS HAVE BEEN EVER CROSSED, IT STANDS AS AN EDICT IN DESTINY.

I HAVE A WIDOW AUNT. FROM ATHENS IS HER HOUSE REMOTE SEVEN LEAGUES.

THERE, GENTLE HERMIA, MAY I MARRY THEE, AND TO THAT PLACE THE SHARP ATHENIAN LAW CANNOT PURSUE US.

HERMIA!

At the home of Peter Quince, the Mechanicals prepare their play.

OUR PLAY IS *THE MOST LAMENTABLE COMEDY AND MOST CRUEL DEATH OF PYRAMUS AND THISBE*.
YOU, NICK BOTTOM, ARE SET DOWN FOR PYRAMUS.

FRANCIS FLUTE, YOU MUST TAKE THISBE ON YOU.
NO, NO. YOU MUST PLAY PYRAMUS!
LET ME PLAY THISBE TOO!
SNUG THE JOINER, YOU, THE LION'S PART.

LET ME PLAY THE LION TOO.
YOU CAN PLAY NO PART BUT PYRAMUS. FOR PYRAMUS IS A MOST LOVELY, GENTLEMANLIKE MAN.
TOMORROW NIGHT, MEET ME IN THE PALACE WOOD. THERE WILL WE REHEARSE!

ACT II

In the forest, just outside of Athens...

ILL MET BY MOONLIGHT, PROUD TITANIA.

WHAT, JEALOUS OBERON? FAIRIES, SKIP HENCE. I HAVE FORSWORN HIS BED AND COMPANY.

AM NOT I THY LORD?

THEN I MUST BE THY LADY. BUT THE BOUNCING AMAZON, YOUR WARRIOR LOVE, TO THESEUS MUST BE WEDDED.

HOW CANST THOU THUS FOR SHAME, TITANIA, KNOWING I KNOW THY LOVE TO THESEUS?

THESE ARE THE FORGERIES OF JEALOUSY. EVILS COME FROM OUR DEBATE.

MY GENTLE PUCK, COME HITHER.
FETCH ME THAT FLOWER; THE HERB I SHOWED THEE ONCE. MAIDENS CALL IT 'LOVE-IN-IDLENESS.'
THE JUICE OF IT, ON SLEEPING EYELIDS LAID, WILL MAKE MAN OR WOMAN MADLY DOTE UPON THE NEXT LIVE CREATURE THAT IT SEES.

I LOVE THEE NOT: THEREFORE PURSUE ME NOT.

YOU DRAW ME! LEAVE YOU YOUR POWER TO DRAW, AND I SHALL HAVE NO POWER TO FOLLOW YOU.

HAST THOU THE FLOWER THERE? WELCOME, WANDERER.
AYE, THERE IT IS.
TAKE THOU SOME OF IT AND SEEK THROUGH THIS GROVE: A SWEET ATHENIAN LADY IS IN LOVE WITH A DISDAINFUL YOUTH. ANOINT HIS EYES.
FEAR NOT, MY LORD. YOUR SERVANT SHALL DO SO.
WHAT THOU SEEST WHEN THOU DOST WAKE, DO IT FOR THY TRUE LOVE TAKE.
WAKE WHEN SOME VILE THING IS NEAR!

Meanwhile...
I HAVE FORGOT OUR WAY. WE'LL REST US, HERMIA, IF YOU THINK IT GOOD. AND TARRY FOR THE COMFORT OF THE DAY.
BE IT SO, LYSANDER.
FIND YOU OUT A BED, FOR I UPON THIS BANK WILL REST MY HEAD.
HERE IS MY BED. SLEEP GIVE THEE ALL HIS REST!
Soon...
THROUGH THE FOREST HAVE I GONE, BUT ATHENIAN FOUND I NONE. NIGHT AND SILENCE!
WHO IS HERE? WEEDS OF ATHENS HE DOTH WEAR.
UPON THY EYES I THROW ALL THE POWER THIS CHARM DOTH OWE.

But then...

BUT WHO IS HERE? LYSANDER, IF YOU LIVE, GOOD SIR, AWAKE.

AND RUN THROUGH FIRE I WILL FOR THY SWEET SAKE!

DO NOT SAY SO, LYSANDER! O, THAT A LADY, OF ONE MAN REFUSED, SHOULD OF ANOTHER THEREFORE BE ABUSED!

# ACT III

And as the Mechanicals practice in the woods, Titania sleeps nearby...

STAY THOU BUT HERE A WHILE.

WHY DO THEY RUN AWAY? THIS IS A KNAVERY OF THEM TO MAKE ME AFEARD.
COME BACK, GOOD FELLOWS!
WHAT ANGEL WAKES ME FROM MY FLOWERY BED?
THY FAIR VIRTUE'S FORCE PERFORCE DOTH MOVE ME TO SWEAR, I LOVE THEE.
METHINKS, MISTRESS, YOU SHOULD HAVE LITTLE REASON FOR THAT. AND YET, REASON AND LOVE KEEP LITTLE COMPANY TOGETHER NOWADAYS.

I AM A SPIRIT OF NO COMMON RATE, AND I DO LOVE THEE. THEREFORE GO WITH ME. I'LL GIVE THEE FAIRIES TO ATTEND ON THEE.
Nearby...
HOW NOW, MAD SPIRIT?
MY MISTRESS WITH A MONSTER IS IN LOVE.
BUT HAST THOU YET LATCHED THE ATHENIAN'S EYES WITH THE LOVE JUICE?
I TOOK HIM SLEEPING. THAT IS FINISHED TOO.
STAND CLOSE. THIS IS THE SAME ATHENIAN.
THIS IS THE WOMAN, BUT NOT THIS THE MAN.

O, WHY REBUKE YOU HIM THAT LOVES YOU SO?

WHAT'S THIS TO MY LYSANDER? AH, GOOD DEMETRIUS, WILT THOU GIVE HIM ME?

THERE IS NO FOLLOWING HER IN THIS FIERCE VEIN.

IF FOR HIS TENDER HERE I MAKE SOME STAY.

THOU HAST MISTAKEN QUITE! ABOUT THE WOOD GO SWIFTER THAN THE WIND, AND HELENA OF ATHENS LOOK THOU FIND.
I GO, I GO! LOOK HOW I GO!
WHEN HIS LOVE HE DOTH ESPY, LET HER SHINE. WHEN THOU WAKEST, IF SHE BE BY, BEG OF HER FOR REMEDY.

Puck returns with Helena and Lysander...
CAPTAIN OF OUR FAIRY BAND, HELENA IS HERE AT HAND, AND THE YOUTH, MISTOOK BY ME, PLEADING FOR A LOVER'S FEE. LORD, WHAT FOOLS THESE MORTALS BE!
YOU DO ADVANCE YOUR CUNNING MORE AND MORE! WHEN I AM SURE YOU HATE ME WITH YOUR HEARTS.
WHY SHOULD YOU THINK THAT I SHOULD WOO IN SCORN?
?!

O HELENA, PERFECT, DIVINE!
TO WHAT, MY LOVE, SHALL I COMPARE THINE EYNE?
YOU ARE UNKIND, DEMETRIUS. IN HERMIA'S LOVE I YIELD YOU UP MY PART. AND YOURS OF HELENA TO ME BEQUEATH.
LYSANDER, KEEP THY HERMIA. I WILL NONE.
IF E'ER I LOVED HER, ALL THAT LOVE IS GONE. MY HEART NOW TO HELENA IS IT HOME RETURNED, THERE TO REMAIN.
NEVER DID MOCKERS WASTE MORE IDLE BREATH!

WHAT LOVE COULD PRESS LYSANDER FROM MY SIDE?
COULD NOT THIS MAKE THEE KNOW, THE HATE I BEAR THEE MADE ME LEAVE THEE SO?
LO, SHE IS ONE OF THIS CONFEDERACY. NOW I PERCEIVE THEY HAVE CONJOINED ALL THREE TO FASHION THIS FALSE SPORT IN SPITE OF ME.

I SAY I LOVE THEE MORE THAN HE CAN DO.

IF THOU SAY SO, WITHDRAW AND PROVE IT TOO.

LYSANDER, WHERETO TENDS ALL THIS?

HANG OFF, THOU CAT, THOU BURR! VILE THING, LET LOOSE.

WHY ARE YOU GROWN SO RUDE? WHAT CHANGE IS THIS, SWEET LOVE?

YOU THIEF OF LOVE! WHAT, HAVE YOU COME BY NIGHT AND STOLEN MY LOVE'S HEART FROM HIM?

GET YOU GONE, YOU DWARF!

LET HER ALONE. FOR IF THOU DOST INTEND NEVER SO LITTLE SHOW OF LOVE TO HER, THOU SHALT ABY IT.
NOW FOLLOW, IF THOU DAR'ST, TO TRY WHOSE RIGHT, OF THINE OR MINE, IS MOST IN HELENA.
FOLLOW? NAY, I'LL GO WITH THEE, CHEEK BY JOWL.
I WILL NOT TRUST YOU, I, NOR LONGER STAY IN YOUR CURST COMPANY!
I AM AMAZED AND KNOW NOT WHAT TO SAY!

THIS IS THY NEGLIGENCE.
AND SO FAR AM I GLAD IT SO DID SORT AS THIS THEIR JANGLING I ESTEEM A SPORT.
THOU SEEST THESE LOVERS SEEK A PLACE TO FIGHT.
HIE THEREFORE, AND LEAD THESE TESTY RIVALS SO ASTRAY AS ONE COME NOT WITHIN ANOTHER'S WAY.

WHERE ART THOU, PROUD DEMETRIUS? SPEAK THOU NOW.
HERE, VILLAIN. DRAWN AND READY. FOLLOW ME THEN TO PLAINER GROUND.
LYSANDER, SPEAK AGAIN! THOU RUNAWAY, THOU COWARD, ART THOU FLED?
FOLLOW MY VOICE. WE'LL TRY NO MANHOOD HERE.
O WEARY NIGHT. SLEEP, THAT SOMETIMES SHUTS UP SORROW'S EYE, STEAL ME AWHILE FROM MINE OWN COMPANY.

NEVER SO WEARY, NEVER SO IN WOE, I CAN NO FURTHER CRAWL, NO FURTHER GO.
ON THE GROUND SLEEP SOUND.
I'LL APPLY TO YOUR EYE. GENTLE LOVER, REMEDY.
WHEN THOU WAKEST, THOU TAKEST, TRUE DELIGHT IN THE SIGHT OF THY FORMER LADY'S EYE. AND THE COUNTRY PROVERB KNOWN, THAT EVERY MAN SHOULD TAKE HIS OWN.

# ACT IV

Meanwhile in the forest grove...
COME, SIT THEE DOWN UPON THIS FLOWERY BED, WHILE I KISS THY FAIR LARGE EARS, MY GENTLE JOY.
WHAT, WILT THOU HEAR SOME MUSIC, MY SWEET LOVE?
I HAVE A REASONABLE GOOD EAR IN MUSIC.
OR SAY, SWEET LOVE, WHAT THOU DESIREST TO EAT.
METHINKS I HAVE A GREAT DESIRE TO A BOTTLE OF HAY.

I HAVE A VENTUROUS FAIRY THAT SHALL SEEK THE SQUIRREL'S HOARD AND FETCH THEE NEW NUTS.
I PRAY YOU, LET NONE OF YOUR PEOPLE STIR ME. I HAVE AN EXPOSITION OF SLEEP COME UPON ME.
SLEEP THOU, AND I WILL WIND THEE IN MY ARMS. O, HOW I LOVE THEE!

SEEST THOU THIS SWEET SIGHT? HER DOTAGE NOW I DO BEGIN TO PITY.
I WILL UNDO THIS HATEFUL IMPERFECTION OF HER EYES.
NOW, MY TITANIA, WAKE YOU, MY SWEET QUEEN.
MY OBERON, WHAT VISIONS HAVE I SEEN! METHOUGHT I WAS ENAMORED OF A DONKEY.

SOUND, MUSIC! COME, MY QUEEN, TAKE HANDS WITH ME. AND ROCK THE GROUND WHEREON THESE SLEEPERS BE.
RESTORE BOTTOM'S HEAD.

NOW WHEN THOU WAKEST, WITH THINE OWN FOOL'S EYES PEEP.
FAIRY KING, ATTEND AND MARK. I DO HEAR THE MORNING LARK.
COME MY LORD, AND IN OUR FLIGHT TELL ME HOW IT CAME THIS NIGHT THAT I SLEEPING HERE WAS FOUND WITH THESE MORTALS ON THE GROUND.

MY LORD, THIS IS MY DAUGHTER HERE. AND THIS, LYSANDER. THIS DEMETRIUS IS. THIS HELENA. I WONDER OF THEIR BEING HERE TOGETHER.

I CANNOT TRULY SAY HOW I CAME HERE. I CAME WITH HERMIA HITHER. OUR INTENT WAS TO BE GONE FROM ATHENS.

ENOUGH, ENOUGH, MY LORD! THEY WOULD HAVE STOL'N AWAY, THEY WOULD, DEMETRIUS.

THE OBJECT AND THE PLEASURE OF MINE EYE, IS ONLY HELENA.

FAIR LOVERS, YOU ARE FORTUNATELY MET. EGEUS, I WILL OVERBEAR YOUR WILL. THESE COUPLES SHALL ETERNALLY BE KNIT. AWAY WITH US TO ATHENS!

ACT V
I HAVE HAD A DREAM. I WILL GET PETER QUINCE TO WRITE A BALLAD OF THIS DREAM.
Soon, Bottom reaches Quince's home.
WHERE ARE THESE LADS? WHERE ARE THESE HEARTS?
BOTTOM! O MOST COURAGEOUS DAY! O MOST HAPPY HOUR!
MASTERS, THE DUKE HAS DINED. MEET PRESENTLY AT THE PALACE; OUR PLAY IS PREFERRED.

At the Palace of Duke Theseus...
'TIS STRANGE, MY THESEUS, THAT THESE LOVERS SPEAK OF.
I NEVER MAY BELIEVE THESE ANTIQUE FABLES NOR THESE FAIRY TOYS.
BUT ALL THEIR MINDS TRANSFIGURED SO TOGETHER, MORE WITNESSETH THAN FANCY'S IMAGES.

HERE COME THE LOVERS, FULL OF JOY AND MIRTH.

JOY, GENTLE FRIENDS! WHERE IS OUR USUAL MANAGER OF MIRTH? IS THERE NO PLAY?

WE WILL HEAR IT. FOR NEVER ANYTHING CAN BE AMISS WHEN SIMPLENESS AND DUTY TENDER IT.

IN THIS SAME INTERLUDE IT DOTH BEFALL THAT I, ONE SNOUT BY NAME, PRESENT A WALL. AND SUCH A WALL, AS I WOULD HAVE YOU THINK, THAT HAD IN IT A CRANNIED HOLE, OR CHINK.
PYRAMUS! PYRAMUS!

I SEE A VOICE! I CAN HEAR MY THISBE'S FACE!

IT IS THE WITTIEST PARTITION THAT EVER I HEARD DISCOURSE, MY LORD.
THIS IS THE SILLIEST STUFF THAT EVER I HEARD.
'TIS ALMOST FAIRY TIME. I FEAR WE SHALL OUTSLEEP THE COMING MORN. SWEET FRIENDS, TO BED.
HAND IN HAND WITH FAIRY GRACE WILL WE SING AND BLESS THIS PLACE. 
NOW UNTIL THE BREAK OF DAY THROUGH THIS HOUSE EACH FAIRY STRAY. AND THE OWNER OF IT BE BLEST EVER SHALL IN SAFETY REST.

IF WE SHADOWS HAVE OFFENDED, THINK BUT THIS, AND ALL IS MENDED! THAT YOU HAVE BUT SLUMBERED HERE WHILE THESE VISIONS DID APPEAR. GIVE ME YOUR HANDS, IF WE BE FRIENDS, AND ROBIN SHALL RESTORE AMENDS.
The End

# Discussion Questions

1. To a modern reader, Egeus's reaction to Hermia's rejection of Demetrius as a spouse may seem extreme. Why do you think Egeus reacted as he did?

2. Helena betrays Hermia and Lysander by revealing their marriage plan to Demetrius. Do you think her reason for doing so was a good one?

3. Fairies cause mischief, and Puck enjoys doing so. Do you think Puck spread the magic flower's juice on Lysander's eyes in Act II by accident? Why would he risk Oberon's wrath by assuming Lysander was Demetrius?

4. When Titania awakens and sees Bottom, she immediately falls in love, even though he has the head of a donkey. What does this say about love?

5. At the end of the play, Theseus overrides Egeus's demand that Hermia marry Demetrius and allows her to marry Lysander. Why do you think he did this?

# Fun Facts

- Almost all Uranus's moons are named after Shakespearean characters. Three of them are from *A Midsummer Night's Dream*: Oberon, Titania, and Puck.

- *A Midsummer Night's Dream* is considered one of Shakespeare's best comedies.

- *A Midsummer Night's Dream* was written about the same time as *Romeo and Juliet*, but this play makes light of love and romance stories.

- In 1840, Madame Lucia Vestris produced the comedy and played the role of Oberon. This started a custom of women playing Oberon and Puck.

- The famous "Wedding March" was written by Felix Mendelssohn for the play in 1842.

# About Shakespeare

Records show William Shakespeare was baptized at Holy Trinity Church in Stratford-upon-Avon, England, on April 26, 1564. There were few birth records at the time, but Shakespeare's birthday is commonly recognized as April 23 of that year. His middle-class parents were John Shakespeare and Mary Arden. John was a tradesman who made gloves.

William most likely went to grammar school, but he did not go to university. He married Anne Hathaway in 1582, and they had three children: Susanna and twins Hamnet and Judith. Shakespeare was in London by 1592 working as an actor and playwright. He began to stand out for his writing. Later in his career, he partly owned the Globe Theater in London, and he was known throughout England.

To mark Shakespeare and his colleagues' success, King James I (reigned 1603–1625) named their theater company King's Men—a great honor. Shakespeare returned to Stratford in his retirement and died April 23, 1616. He was 52 years old.

# Famous Phrases

*The course of true love never did run smooth.*

*I know a bank where the wild thyme blows,*
*Where oxlips and the nodding violet grows.*

*Lord, what fools these mortals be!*

*Love looks not with the eyes, but with the mind,*
*And therefore is winged Cupid painted blind.*

*Never did mockers waste more idle breath!*

# Glossary

**dote** - to show affection.

**edict** - an order or demand.

**enamored** - in love with.

**eyne** - a spelling of eyes that is used for rhyme.

**girdle round about the earth** - cover the earth searching.

**glade** - an open space surrounded by woods.

**henchman** - a page to a person of high rank.

**hither** - to this place.

**knavery** - being deceitful.

**league** - a measurement of distance.

**love-in-idleness** - the name for a pansy.

**negligence** - showing carelessness.

**nuptial hour** - time of our wedding.

**weed** - clothing.

# Additional Works by Shakespeare

**Romeo and Juliet (1594–96)**

**A Midsummer Night's Dream (1595–96)**

The Merchant of Venice (1596-97)

Much Ado About Nothing (1598–99)

**Hamlet (1599–1601)**

Twelfth Night (1600–02)

**Othello (1603–04)**

**King Lear (1605–06)**

**Macbeth (1606–07)**

The Tempest (1610-11)

• Bold titles are available in this set of Shakespeare Illustrated Classics.

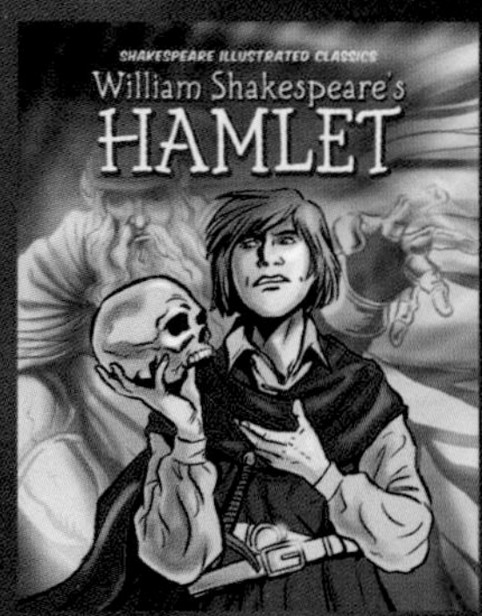

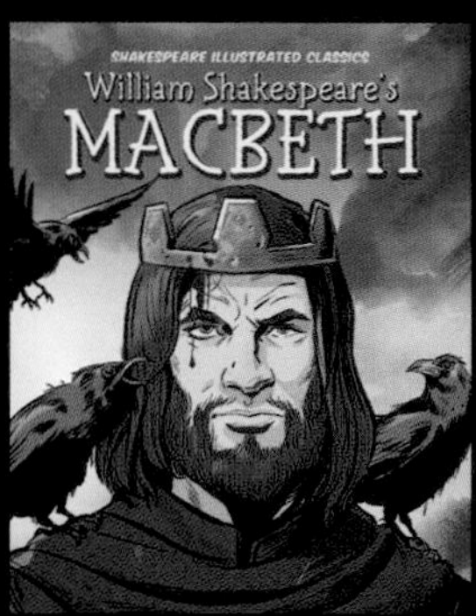

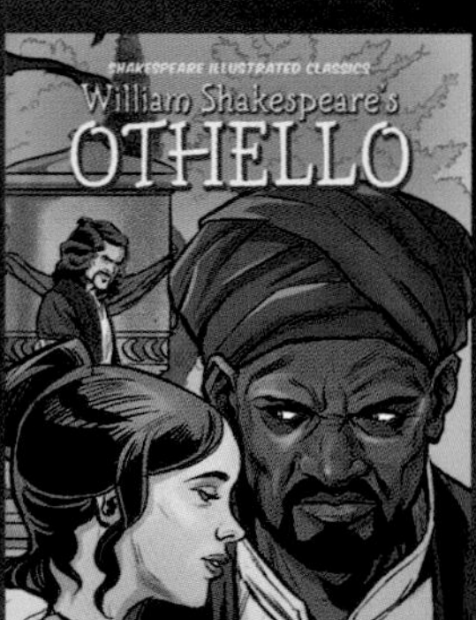

**Booklinks**

NONFICTION NETWORK

FREE! ONLINE NONFICTION RESOURCES

To learn more about SHAKESPEARE, visit **abdobooklinks.com** or scan this QR code. These links are routinely monitored and updated to provide the most current information available.